DC™

SUPER-PETS!

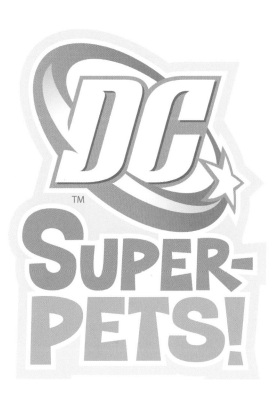

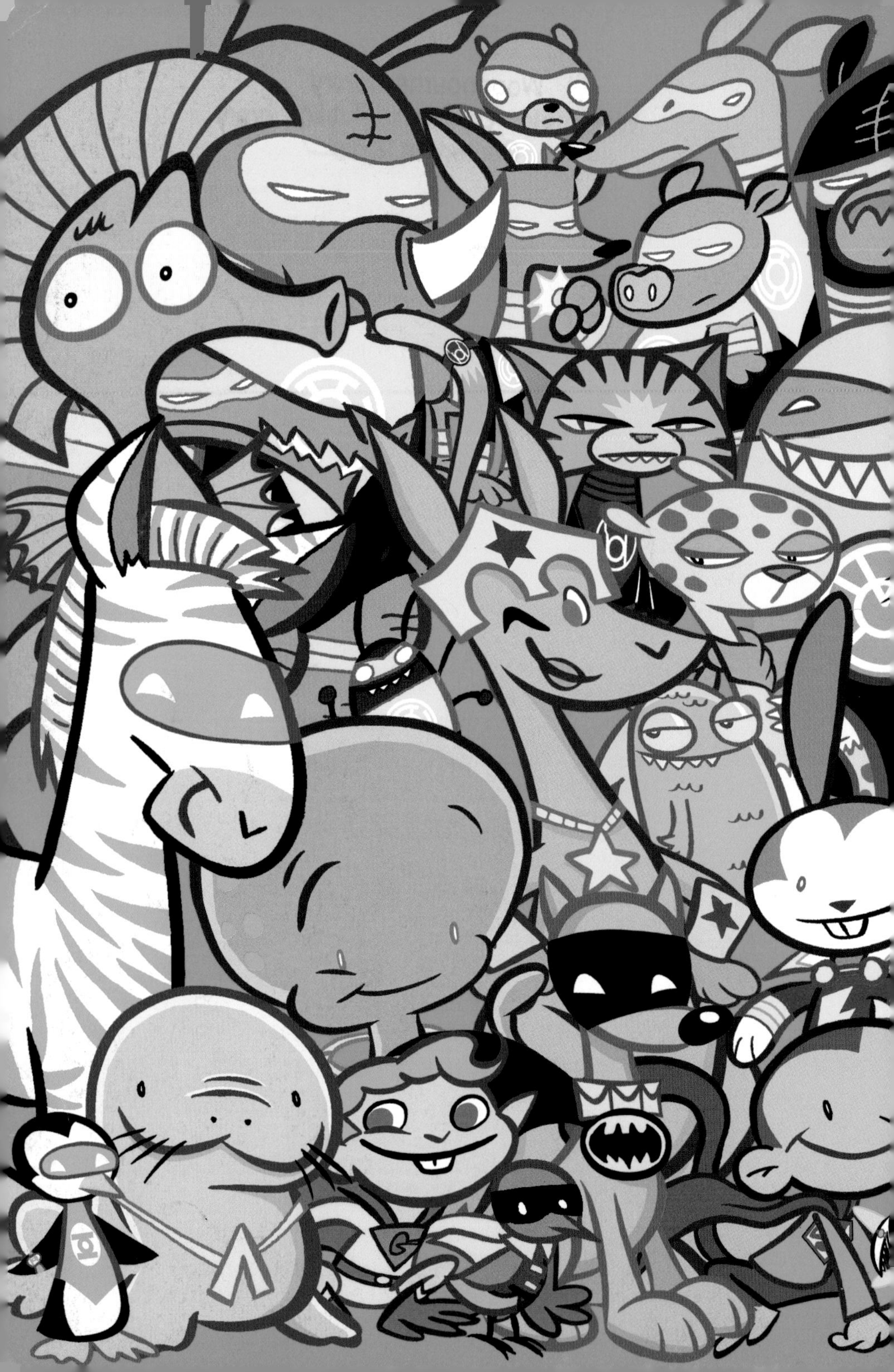

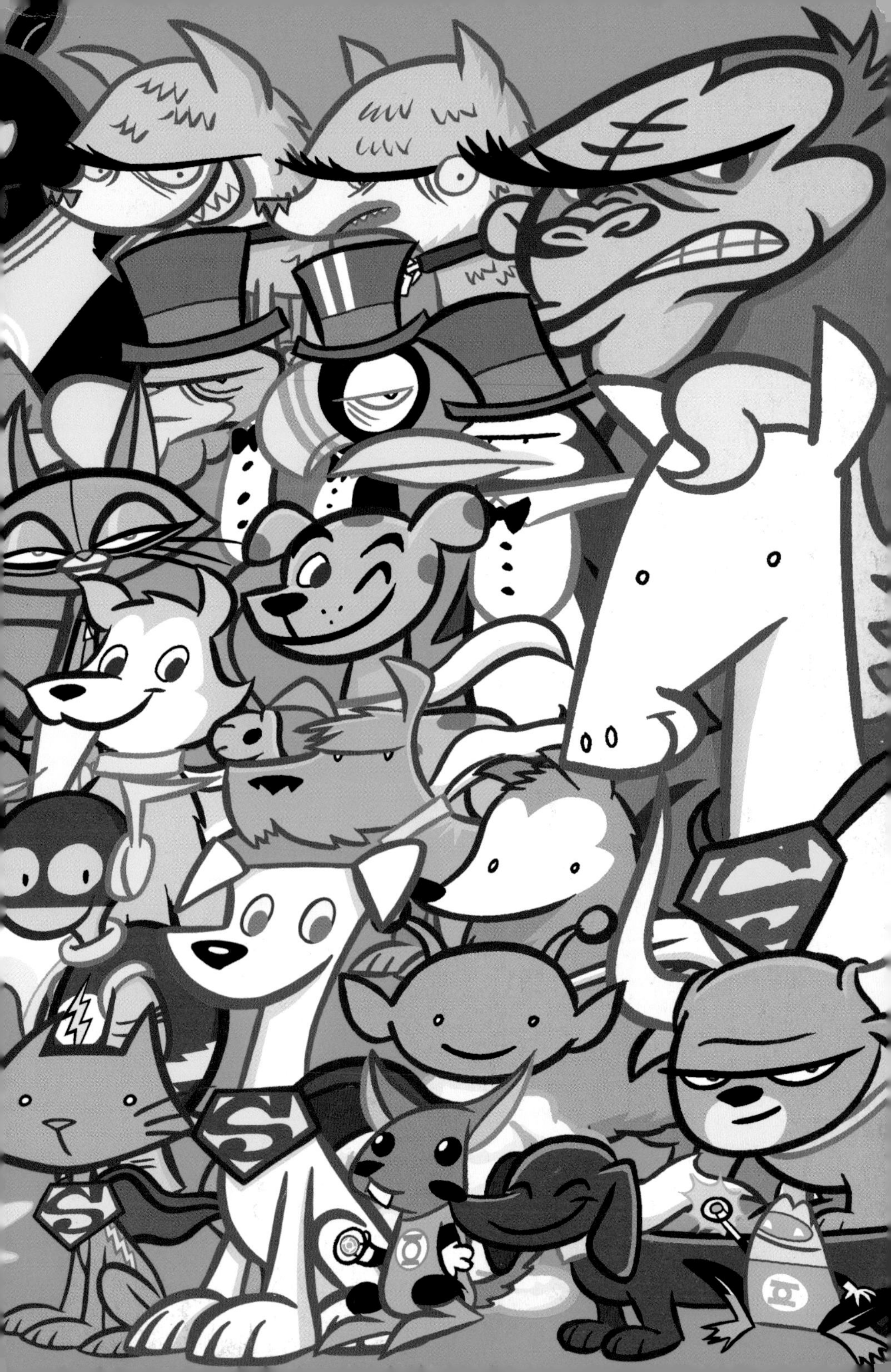

DC™

SUPER-PETS!

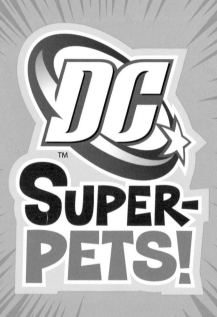

by J.E. Bright

THE FASTEST PET ON EARTH

illustrated by
Art Baltazar

Wonder Woman created by
William Moulton Marston

Picture Window Books™
a capstone imprint

# Starring...

## JUMPA
### THE KANGA!

## CHAUNCEY
### THE CHEETAH!

## WONDER WOMAN!

# TABLE OF CONTENTS!

## SUPER-PET HERO FILE 010:
# JUMPA

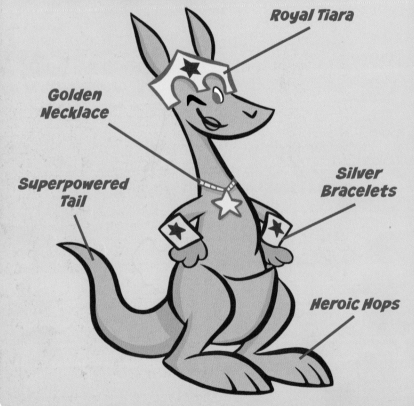

Royal Tiara

Golden Necklace

Superpowered Tail

Silver Bracelets

Heroic Hops

**Species:** Kanga

**Place of Birth:** Paradise Island

**Age:** Unknown

**Favorite Food:** Jumping Beans

**Bio:** Kangas are found only on Paradise Island. Like kangaroos, kangas can leap long distances, but they're also super-speedy. These heroic hoppers are the royal rides of Wonder Woman and other Amazons.

# Chapter 1

# THE GOLDEN TORTOISE

**Jumpa** carried **Wonder Woman** through the jungles of Paradise Island. It was the young kanga's second time on patrol as the super hero's steed. Jumpa had taken over the job from her mother, who had been asked to guard the Amazons' main temple.

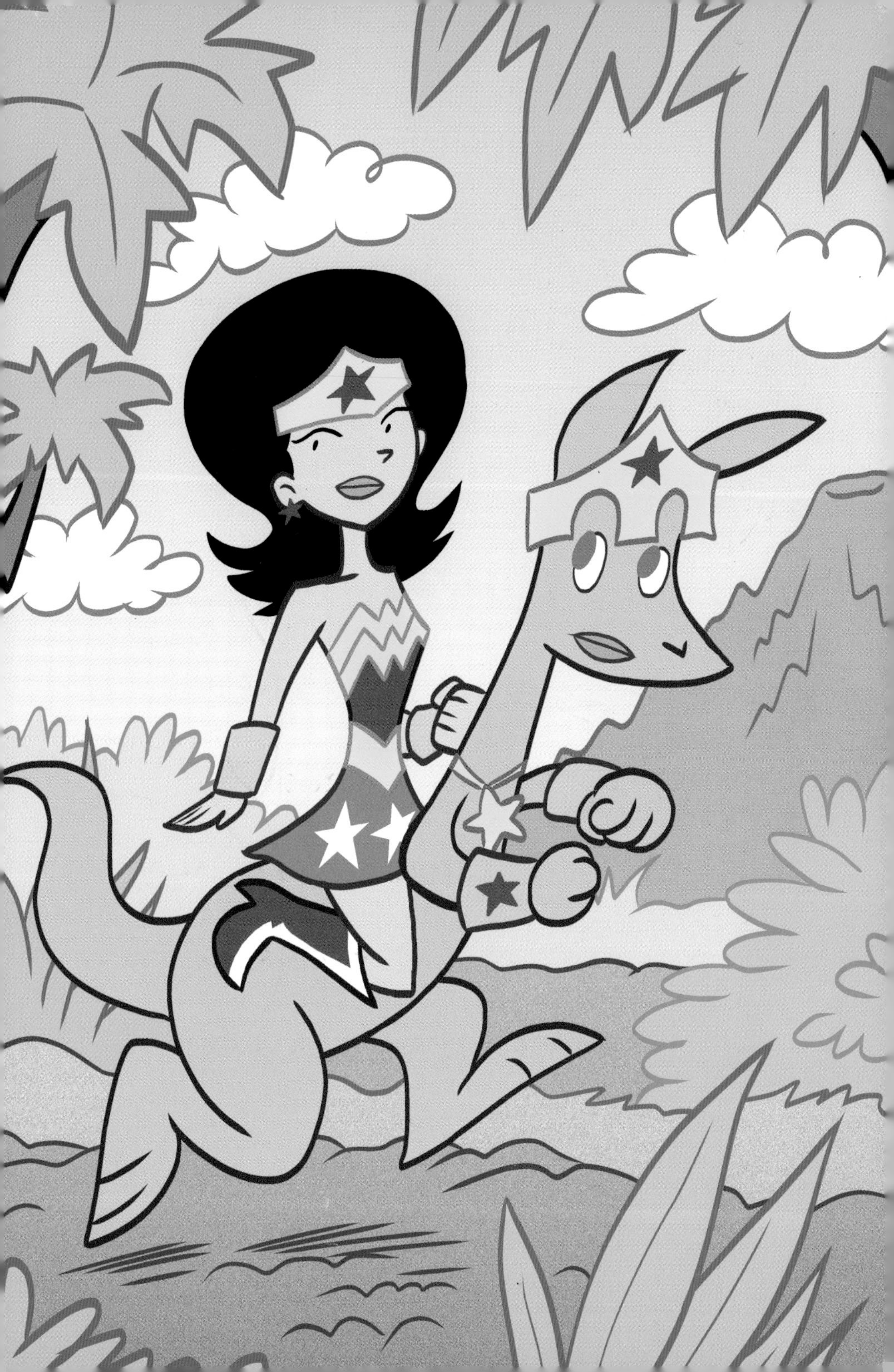

"One quick tour through the Sacred Grove, Jumpa," Wonder Woman said. "Then we'll wrap up tonight's patrol with a pass across Coral Shore."

Jumpa nodded and sped off toward the Grove. *WOOOSH!*

Like the smaller kangaroos from the mainland, kangas were built for jumping. But unlike Jumpa's kangaroo cousins, she didn't hop to get around. Instead, she ran on her powerful legs like a speedy dinosaur.

While Jumpa zipped along the edge of the Grove, Wonder Woman watched the trees for danger. "We've gotten reports that the villain Cheetah escaped her prison," the super hero said. **"I believe that she will be causing trouble soon."**

"All is well here," Wonder Woman said. She tugged Jumpa's reins. She led the kanga in another direction. "To the shore!"

ZOOMM!

Jumpa looked up at the tallest peak on the island. At the summit stood a temple where Jumpa's mother was on guard duty. Jumpa hoped that one day she might become a guard like her mother. However, she still felt too young for her own job as Wonder Woman's steed.

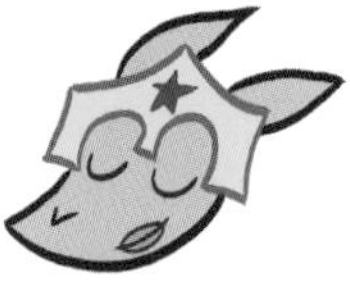

Soon, they arrived at Coral Shore. Jumpa sped onto the sand, which glowed pink in the setting sun.

**"Snort!"** Jumpa sounded her alarm. She spotted a domed shape moving along the shoreline. Something was digging into the sand.

**"Easy,"** Wonder Woman whispered. **"I see it, too. Let's get a better look."**

Jumpa crept closer. The creature had a brown shell and flippers. It was lying next to a shallow hole.

"Oh!" Wonder Woman shouted in surprise. "It's a tortoise! **Look, Jumpa, her eggs have hatched!"**

Jumpa saw that the mother tortoise was protecting a group of ten babies. The little ones flopped around, playing on the sand.

Then a pile of three baby tortoises shifted and revealed a bright flash.

Wonder Woman and Jumpa gasped.

**One of the babies was pure gold!**

**"A golden tortoise,"** said Wonder Woman. "The only place they're ever born is here on Paradise Island. This special baby is the first I've ever seen."

Wonder Woman kneeled near the babies. She reached for the gold one.

# CLAMP!

The tiny tortoise snapped his beak

shut. Wonder Woman quickly pulled

her hand back. She laughed.

**"Strong, isn't he?"** said Jumpa.

"A golden tortoise can boost the powers of anyone touching him," replied the Amazon Princess. "Some people would do terrible things to have this creature. I must ask the other Amazons how to protect him."

"It's getting dark. I won't be back from the temple until morning," said Wonder Woman. "I'm counting on you to guard these tortoises."

With great pride, Jumpa raised her head high and nodded. **"I would be honored,"** the Super-Pet said.

"Good luck, my friend," said Wonder Woman. **"Watch out for Cheetah. If she steals the golden tortoise, the whole world will be in danger."** Then the super hero ran off through the Sacred Grove.

Soon after, night fell over Paradise Island. The golden tortoise's shell sparkled in the bright moonlight. Jumpa reached out her tail to him, yanking it back when he snapped.

**"I'm giving you the nickname**

**Oro,"** Jumpa told the golden tortoise.

Oro flapped his flippers with

excitement. Jumpa reached out her tail

again. She whipped it away when he

tried to bite. **"Snap!"** she said.

By repeating **"Snap!"** every time Oro chomped at her tail, Jumpa trained the smart critter to bite on command.

As the night dragged on, Oro and the other tortoises fell asleep. Jumpa sat quietly beside them. The Super-Pet looked down the shoreline. She checked the beach again. Not far away, a pair of **yellow eyes** glowed back at her through the darkness.

**"Oh no!"** the kanga said. Jumpa hopped to her feet. She saw a large cat racing toward her.

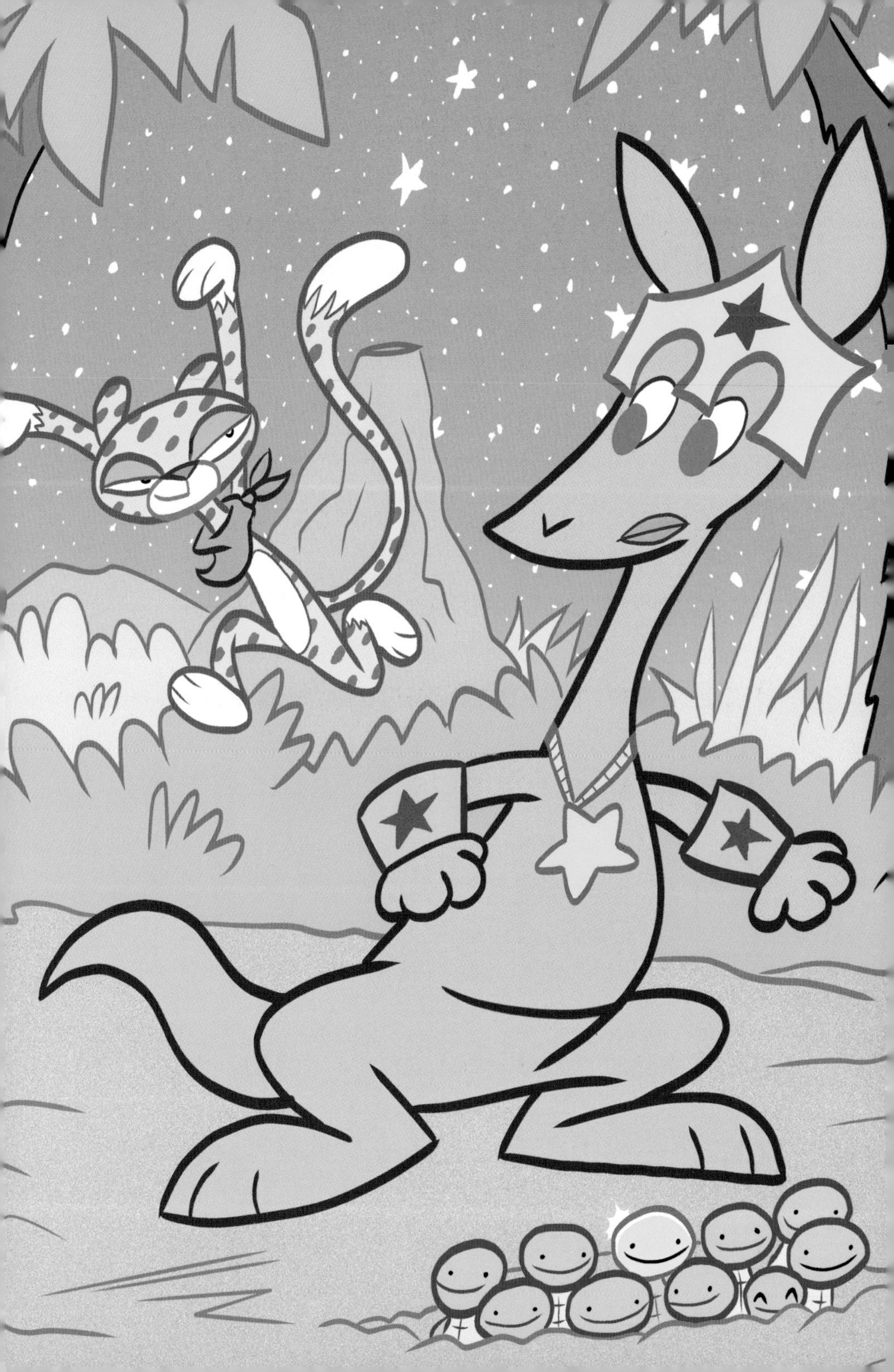

# Chapter 2

# CAT BURGLAR

Jumpa crouched in fighting position in front of the tortoises. As the cat got closer, she saw its thin body and brown spots. **"A cheetah!"** Jumpa said.

The cat moved closer. "Hello, dear," the cheetah said. **"My name is Chauncey.** And who might you be?"

"**I'm Jumpa**," the Super-Pet replied.
"**Don't come any closer!**"

Chauncey smiled and sat down. He eyed the tortoises and licked his lips. "I'm glad to see my time is paying off," said the evil cheetah. "I've been waiting for a golden tortoise to hatch for such a long time. When I take it back to my mistress, **Cheetah,** she's going to be so pleased with me."

"There's no way you're taking the golden tortoise to Cheetah!" Jumpa growled. "*I'll never let you!*"

"Oh, relax," Chauncey said. "You don't have to shout." He turned around, and for a second, Jumpa hoped the evil cat would leave.

Then suddenly, Chauncey kicked out his hind legs, scattering sand into Jumpa's face. FWOOSH!

**"Bleck!"** Jumpa spat, clearing her mouth and wiping at her eyes.

Still blinded, the Super-Pet tried to stay between the tortoises and Chauncey. **WOOOOSH!**

The cat dashed around her. Jumpa sped after him, but the cheetah was too quick. He pounced onto the nest. He scooped Oro into his mouth, gently holding the tortoise between his teeth.

With her vision blurred, **Jumpa leaped at Chauncey.** **BOING!**

The quick cat dashed out of the nest in a flash. Oro's power boost had already given the cheetah super-speed. Jumpa had never seen an animal move so fast. Chauncey waited on the edge of the ocean and laughed.

Then he turned around and sprinted toward the waves.

With the power boost, Chauncey ran so fast that he zoomed over the water. His feet barely touched the ocean's surface. FWOOSH!

Jumpa took a moment to clear her eyes. When she looked up again, she was scared to see that Chauncey had already disappeared.

**"I can't let him get away,"** Jumpa said to herself. For a second, the young kanga thought about rushing to the temple for help. But she had promised to keep the tortoises safe.

Jumpa had powers of her own. **She wouldn't rest until the golden tortoise was back on Paradise Island.**

The young kanga placed the other

tortoises in her pouch. Then she took

a deep breath, narrowed her eyes,

and ran toward the ocean. When she

reached the water's edge, she crouched

down and jumped with all her might.

Jumpa's leap carried her high above

the waves. As the wind whipped in

her face, she spotted a tiny island in

the direction Chauncey was running.

The speedy Super-Pet aimed her body

toward it.

With a hard thump, Jumpa landed

right on the island. She only paused

to take another deep breath before she

leaped again.

Jumping from island to island,

Jumpa followed the cheetah as he sped

across the ocean. But she was losing

sight of Chauncey in the distance.

Jumpa had to catch up somehow —

her jumping wasn't enough.

Jumpa had to try something more daring. Then she heard the whisper of a helicopter.

**FWOOP! FWOOP! FWOOP!**

Jumpa searched for the source of the sound. She spotted a tiny dot of light from the helicopter above. She realized with relief that it was heading in Chauncey's direction.

The cheetah had vanished completely. **The helicopter was Jumpa's only hope.**

Gritting her teeth, Jumpa crouched down. **She leaped higher than she ever had before.**

The Super-Pet soared upward for the helicopter. It was higher than she'd thought. As she got closer, Jumpa worried that she hadn't jumped hard enough. She was slowing down!

Jumpa stretched in the air as the helicopter rushed closer. She reached and barely grabbed onto it.

Jumpa watched the dark ocean below for any sign of Chauncey. With the helicopter moving so quickly through the sky, it didn't take long for her to spot Oro shining below.

Chauncey was sitting beside Oro on the shore of a small island. Even from high above, **Jumpa could see that he was panting hard.** Cheetahs were built for speed but not distance running. He was probably resting.

Jumpa waited until the helicopter was over the island. **Then she let go.**

# Chapter 3

# RACE TO THE FINISH

**Jumpa landed hard on the sand next to Chauncey.** Oro was waddling in circles between the cat's paws. Rolling toward the cheetah, Jumpa grabbed onto his back leg.

Chauncey howled in shock.

**"Let go!"** he screamed.

**"Give me back Oro!"**

Jumpa replied.

**"Dream on!"** Chauncey said. He scooped the golden tortoise up with his mouth. With an extra burst of speed, he tried to pull free.

Jumpa couldn't hang on for long. **"Wait!"** she cried. "You wouldn't be able to beat me in a race without that tortoise's power boost!"

Chauncey stopped struggling. He spat Oro out onto the sand. **"Are you out of your mind?!"** he asked.

"Any cheetah can run faster than a kangaroo," Chauncey said. "Besides, I'm no ordinary cheetah."

"Well, I'm no ordinary kangaroo," Jumpa replied. "I'm a kanga. And I don't think you could beat me."

"Of course I could," said Chauncey.

Jumpa smiled. "Prove it," she said.

"Fine," Chauncey replied. "I will. How shall we do this?"

"We'll race one lap around the island," Jumpa decided. "Whoever circles around the shoreline and gets back to the tortoise first, keeps him."

"How can I be sure you won't cheat?" Chauncey asked.

"I'm a truthful kanga," Jumpa said. "How do I know *you* won't cheat?"

"I've never cheated in my life," Chauncey replied. *"I can't wait to make you eat my dust."*

Jumpa and Chauncey lined up beside one another on the shore. They both crouched down in their ready positions.

*"Get ready,"* Jumpa began. *"Get set. Goooo!"*

They took off running across the hot sand.

Jumpa quickly found out that

the cheetah had incredible speed.

Chauncey pulled ahead as they ran

off the beach. Then they headed into

a wooded area along the waterside.

A race around the island wasn't all about speed. The woods were covered with brush and fallen trees. These items slowed Chauncey down, but Jumpa leaped over them. When the woods ended, she was in the lead.

After the woods, the island flattened out into a long, curving strip of beach. Chauncey pulled ahead again.

But as she peered at the end of the flat beach, **Jumpa smiled.** The beach ended at a wide patch of watery swamp.

**SCREEEECH!!**

Chauncey came grinding to a halt.

The quick cat couldn't run across water

without Oro. **"No fair!"** he whined. **"I**

**hate getting wet!"**

Jumpa didn't even pause.

**BOING!**

She leaped as far as she could.

Although she didn't quite clear the

swamp, it didn't bother her to get her

feet wet and muddy.

**SPA-LOOSH!**

The cheetah was far behind when Jumpa got to the beach where they had left Oro. He couldn't catch up fast enough to beat her.

## Jumpa won the race!

She stood near Oro, panting and smiling. The sun was starting to rise.

Chauncey walked up, his sides heaving. **"Congratulations,"** he said with anger.

**"Thanks,"** Jumpa said. **"Now I'm taking the tortoise back home."**

Suddenly, Chauncey darted to Oro and grabbed the tortoise in his mouth. "No, you're not," he said.

**"I thought you didn't cheat!"** Jumpa shouted.

*HAHAHAHA!* Chauncey laughed, which sounded funny with Oro between his teeth. "I don't mind being a cheating cheetah," he said.

Before Chauncey could start running, Jumpa shouted, **"Snap!"**

CLAMMP!!!

Oro bit down on Chauncey's tongue.

**"Yoooowl!"** Chauncey screamed

and let go of Oro.

Jumpa leaped forward and grabbed

the golden tortoise. She felt a rush of

power through her whole body.

"**Goodbye**," Jumpa told Chauncey.

She crouched and leaped into the air.

With Oro's power boost, Jumpa

jumped so high and fast that she

didn't even need to stop on any boats

or islands on the way. She leaped all

the way back to Paradise Island.

The morning sun streaked colors

across the sky. Jumpa returned Oro

and his brothers and sisters to their

mother, who had returned to the nest.

Jumpa had just sat down when Wonder Woman strode onto the beach. Jumpa explained to Wonder Woman what had happened during the night. The super hero was grateful.

**"Thank you for guarding the tortoises so well,"** Wonder Woman told Jumpa. **"I'm proud of you.** We're going to take the golden tortoise to the temple. He will be presented to Hippolyta, the Queen of the Amazons. **I think you should be the one who brings him to her."**

Jumpa smiled and nodded happily.

**"Thank you,"** said the Super-Pet. She was very proud of herself, too.

Maybe she wasn't too young to be Wonder Woman's steed after all!

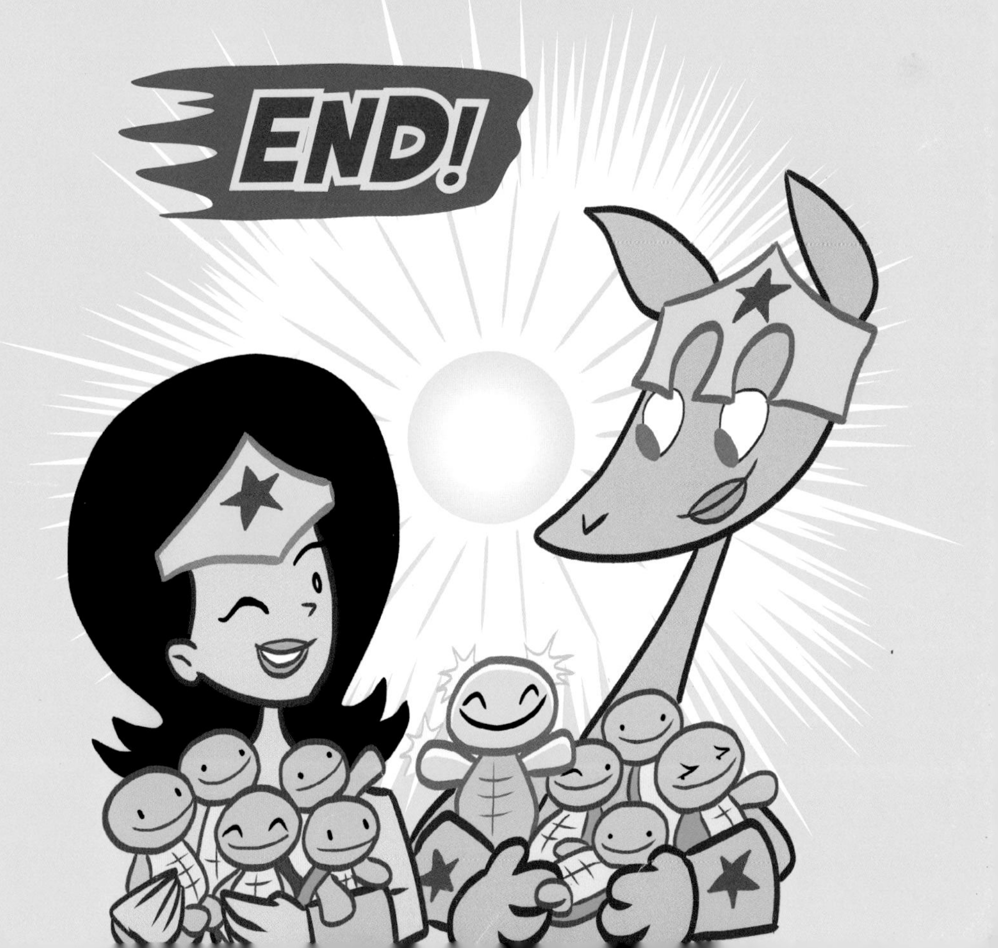
END!

# KNOW YOUR

**Krypto**

**Streaky**

**Beppo**

**Comet**

**Ace**

**Jumpa**

**Whatzit**

**B'dg**

**Storm**

**Topo**

**Ark**

**Hoppy**

**Paw Pooch**

**Bull Dog**

**Chameleon Collie**

**Hot Dog**

Aw yeah, **HERO PETS!**

**Tail Terrier**

**Tusky Husky**

# SUPER-PETS!

**Ignatius**

**Chauncey**

**Crackers**

**Giggles**

**Artie Puffin**

**Griff**

**Waddles**

**Rozz**

**Dex-Starr**

**Glomulus**

**Misty**

**Sneezers**

**Whoosh**

**Pronto**

**Snorrt**

**Rolf**

**Squealer**

**Kajunn**

Aw yeah, **VILLAIN PETS!**

# AW YEAH, JOKES!

Why can't you play cards in the jungle?

Why?!

There are too many cheetahs!

What's a kangaroo's favorite season?

Beats me.

Spring!

What do you get when you cross a cheetah and a hamburger?

I don't know.

Fast food!

# WORD POWER!

**command** (kuh-MAND)—an order to do something

**mainland** (MAYN-luhnd)—the largest part of a country or continent, as opposed to an island

**reins** (RAYNZ)—straps that control a horse or other animal that can be ridden

**steed** (STEED)—a horse, especially an energetic one

**summit** (SUHM-it)—the highest point

**temple** (TEM-puhl)—a building used for worship

**tortoise** (TOR-tuhss)—a turtle, especially one that lives on land

# MEET THE AUTHOR!

## J.E. Bright

J. E. Bright has had more than 50 novels, novelizations, and non-fiction books published for children and young adults. He is a full-time freelance writer, living in a tiny apartment in the SoHo neighborhood of Manhattan with his good, fat cat, Gladys, and his evil cat, Mabel, who is getting fatter.

# MEET THE ILLUSTRATOR!

## Eisner Award-winner Art Baltazar

Art Baltazar is a cartoonist machine from the heart of Chicago! He defines cartoons and comics not only as an art style, but as a way of life. Currently, Art is the creative force behind *The New York Times* best-selling, Eisner Award-winning, DC Comics series Tiny Titans and the co-writer for *Billy Batson and the Magic of SHAZAM!* Art is living the dream! He draws comics and never has to leave the house. He lives with his lovely wife, Rose, big boy Sonny, little boy Gordon, and little girl Audrey. Right on!

# Art Baltazar
## says:

# Read all of the DC SUPER-PETS stories today!

DC SUPER-PETS!
HEROES OF THE HIGH SEAS
by J.E. Bright
Illustrated by Art Baltazar

DC SUPER-PETS!
MIDWAY MONKEY MADNESS
by Sarah Hines Stephens
Illustrated by Art Baltazar

DC SUPER-PETS!
POOCHES OF POWER!
by Sarah Hines Stephens
Illustrated by Art Baltazar

DC SUPER-PETS!
ROYAL RODENT RESCUE
by John Sazaklis
Illustrated by Art Baltazar

DC SUPER-PETS!
SUPER HERO SPLASH DOWN
by Jane Mason
Illustrated by Art Baltazar

DC SUPER-PETS!
THE FASTEST PET ON EARTH
by J.E. Bright
Illustrated by Art Baltazar

## Picture Window Books™

Published in 2011
A Capstone Imprint
151 Good Counsel Drive, P.O. Box 669
Mankato, Minnesota 56002
www.capstonepub.com

Cataloging-in-Publication Data is available at the
Library of Congress website.

ISBN: 978-1-4048-6264-7 (library binding)
ISBN: 978-1-4048-6623-2 (paperback)

Summary: Chauncey the Cheetah is loose
on Paradise Island, but Jumpa the kangaroo
isn't worried.

Art Director & Designer: Bob Lentz
Editor: Donald Lemke
Production Specialist: Michelle Biedscheid
Creative Director: Heather Kindseth
Editorial Director: Michael Dahl
Publisher: Lori Benton

Printed in the United States of America
in Stevens Point, Wisconsin.
072011   006298R

DC™

SUPER-PETS!

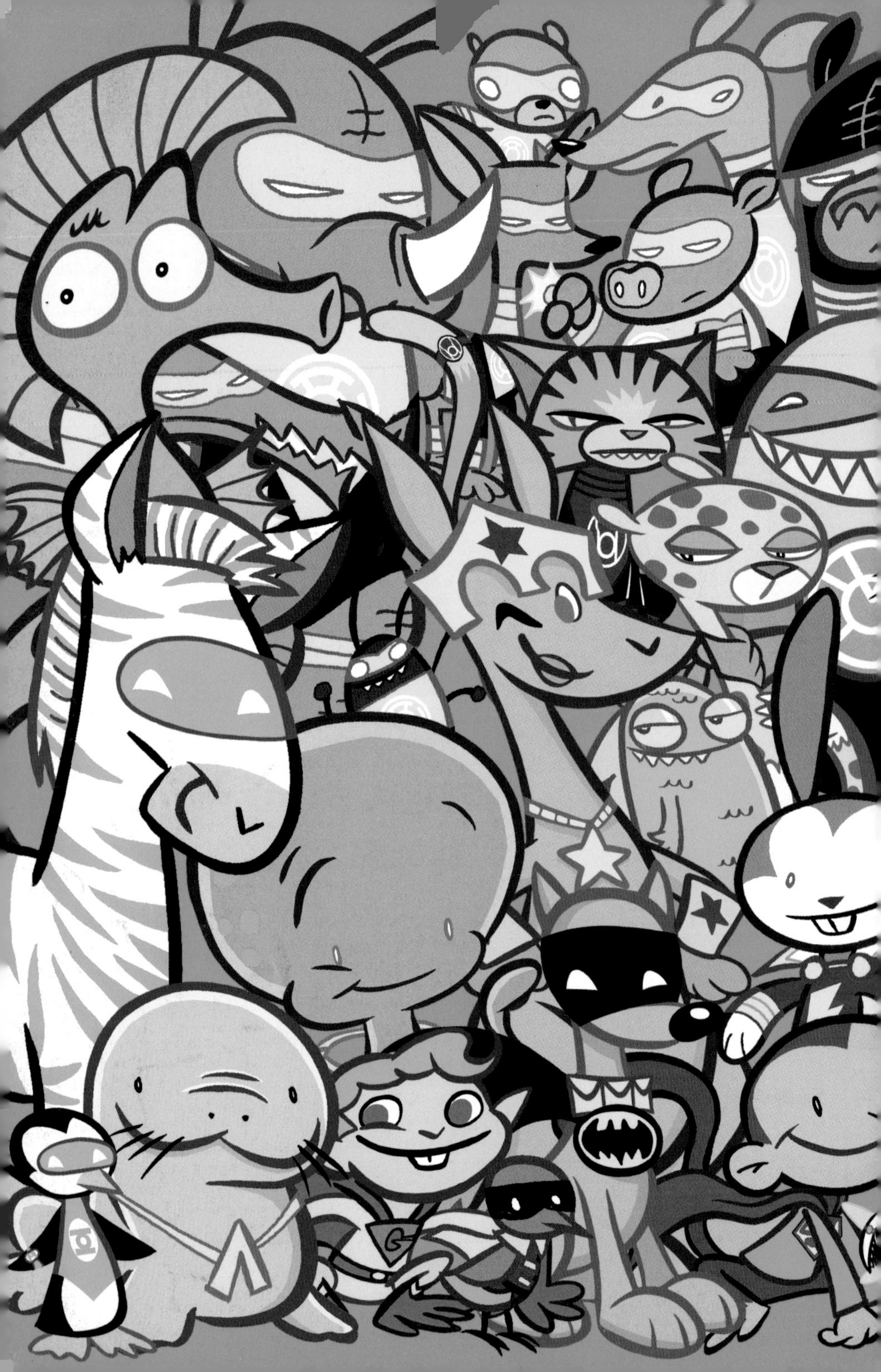

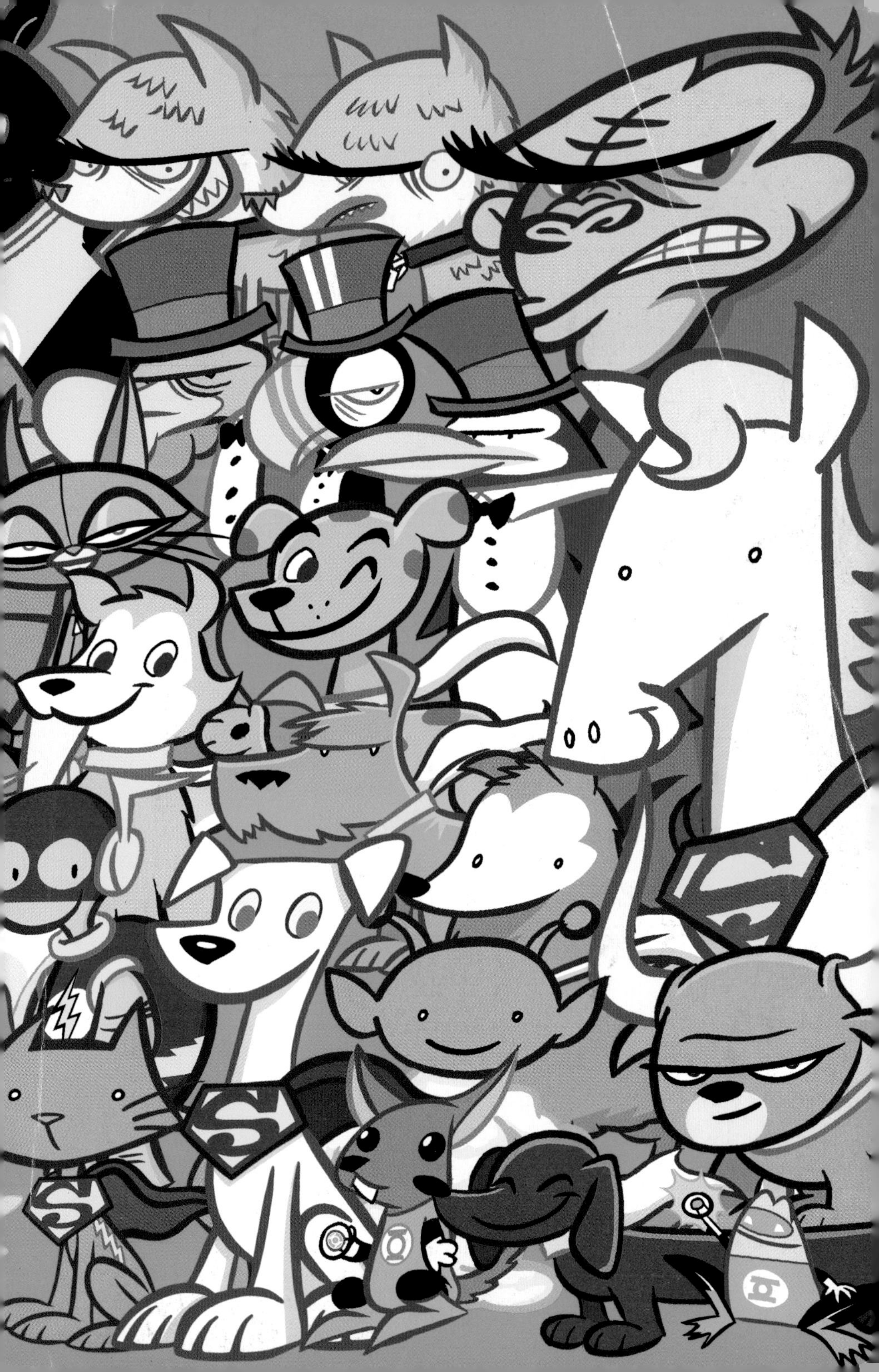

DC™

SUPER-PETS!

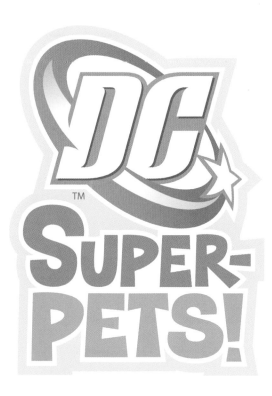